SREEN

Saving the Magic

by
Fay Jones

The Land of SREEN

Grickle Woods

Great Twilk Pass

Grey Lodge Mountains

To Umble Over

Umble Down

Feather Fuzzy Fields

River Tong

High Mill

Rainbow Lake

To Dragon River

Topple End Farm

Dreep Grain

Umble Up

Dedicated to my family,

with much love and thanks.

Chapter 1

A Shocking Fall

The children both sat on the leafy ground with their backs against the knobbly old sweet chestnut tree. They were hungrily tucking into their packed lunches.

'Shhh, what's that noise?' snapped Elvie, pointing at a patch of undergrowth. They could hear a strange buzzing and crackling noise that sounded as if it were coming from the bramble patch next to their den.

'Come on.' Aiden said excitedly. They hurriedly put their food in their bags and jumped up to go and investigate the strange sounds.

Aiden went first, followed by Elvie, who had grabbed both their bags and held them to her chest as if to protect herself from the noise. It felt quite spooky to them, as it was not a noise you would normally hear in the woods. Investigating and holding each other's hands for courage, they crept forwards. Aiden in front, peering to try and see clearly, his head outstretched before him. Puffs of smoke and crackles sounded out in spurts.

'Be careful it's not elect...', but before Elvie could finish her sentence, hand in hand with Aiden and still clutching their bags close to her chest, she was pulled forwards and down by him as they tumbled in a shocking fall through the ground! Instead of being covered in mud and leaves at the bottom of a hole, they had landed somewhere (quite awkwardly) on a pile of unfamiliar feathery fluff!

* * *

Earlier that day, Aiden and Elvie Baldwin had been allowed to play in the woods. Mum had told them to be back within the hour. The children lived on the quiet edge of town in a small terraced house. Behind their row of houses was a secret playing field. At the far edge of the field was some woodland, and in the middle of the field stood a fantastic climbing frame, a slide and some swings. It was so unknown that only the children who lived in the street knew about it – that's why it was so secret – like their own private playground – well, theirs and a few neighbours!

The summer holidays were here at last! Grey clouds made the sky a little dull, but the air was warm and had a summery smell about it. The two children were busily building a den from bits of old tree branches and logs. They had already made a rope swing on the ancient sweet chestnut tree, using their dad's old and dirty towing rope.

'I'm already hungry' said Elvie, as she pulled her backpack towards her and started rifling through it for her packed lunch.

She was eight years old, tidy, and always looked delightful no matter what the occasion. A beautiful girl, tall for her age, with shoulder length curly blond hair and almond shaped hazel coloured eyes, which showed her spirit in their depth. Her oval face and pretty mouth glowed when she smiled, as if the sun shone through her. Life was full of fun and excitement, and every day was to be lived to the full, with dogged determination.

'Me too, my stomach is gnawing at my back bone' laughed Aiden, as he hastily pulled his sandwich from his bag.

He was a typical boy who gave little interest to his appearance – shorts and T-shirt were his usual – even in the middle of winter. He too had curly hair but it was fair, short and wavy, and usually tousled, even after just being brushed. His broad, handsome, smiley face and round hazel eyes with their cheeky brightness, gave him huge charisma. At ten years old he was full of excitement and purpose. Also tall for his age, you could see he would grow to be a strong man.

They both felt happy to be on holiday and blissfully unaware of what was just about to happen to them. Their lives were about to change forever!

Chapter 2

Everything Is Different

Without knowing how their day was going to end, Aiden was already wishing he had worn long sleeves and jeans. His muddy arms and legs were now covered in this feathery mess!

'Ahh! Ouch!' they exclaimed, more from the shock of the fall than the landing!

'What happened? Are you OK?' asked Elvie. Aiden, who was the oldest, was trying to sound upbeat rather than worried when he replied.

'Yes, I'm fine. You?' They both looked at each other, puzzled and bewildered, as they clambered down to the ground from the pile of strange feathery fluff Brushing it from their clothes, they noticed that everything around them was different – brighter, more colourful, odd, and at this moment, very feathery!

'Perft-perft,' Elvie spat feathers from her mouth, 'what is all of this fluff?' she said pulling some from her lip.

'It must be some kind of crop!' stated Aiden, noticing more piles dotted around them like loose bales of hay. These appeared to have been placed, waiting for collection. They had been left randomly amongst the stubbly rooted ground in-between the uncut tall swaying featherlike grass. This strange grass was twice the height of the children, and feathery from half way up its stems to the top.

Looking around, they noticed some unusual gnarled and rustic wooden huts or houses, perhaps the size of a small shed or large dog kennel. These were purposefully built in groups, with narrow dusty lanes dividing the clusters of huts. Small metal farm tools lay scattered about the place. The landscape was simply stunning, with intensely coloured bright green and yellow fields gently undulating away into the distance. Vivid coloured flowers carpeted the meadows close by.

'I can't take it all in,' gasped Elvie, her eyes open wide and her head glancing about. 'We're in a – a different land!' she said, stuttering and still wiping feathery fluff from her face with her sleeve.

'THE LAND OF SREEN TO BE PRECISE!' shouted an angry voice. 'AND YOU'VE JUST RUINED MY BALE OF FEATHER FUZZY!' It said pointing to the pile the children had landed on.

Aiden, by now, was dumbstruck. His jaw dropped open, and all that would come out of his mouth was a gasp!

Walking towards them was an extremely unusual creature. It walked upright like a man and was very thin. So thin that they thought he almost disappeared at one point. It was about three feet tall, with long slender limbs and was wearing dusty bright green trousers and a tatty purple round necked top, which hung shabbily from his shoulders.

Its hands and feet appeared larger than they ought to be, as he stamped his purple slippered foot and swiped his fist angrily through the air at the children. Its head was elongated, which made its deep-set green eyes look very close together. The ears were small, but its mouth and jaw were large and angular with quite thick lips. Skin fell in folds and wrinkles around its cheeks, showing it probably had some age, but.... what a nose!! Long and narrow from the eyebrows and splaying out to make a huge bobble at the end above its thick top lip!

'A FAIRY!' Elvie shouted excitedly.

'Ugly fairy!' thought Aiden, unsure whether to turn and run or stay and protect his sister.

'MOOZE DUNG!' retorted the thing angrily.

'The very thought of it. A fairy I am not!' It said indignantly. 'I am a Twilk, and I take it you are humans?'

Finding the courage to speak, Aiden spurted out quickly and uncontrollably. 'Yes we are – *how* do you know that?' and stepping in front of Elvie as if to shield her he added abruptly, '*Where* are we? – and *what on earth* is a Twilk?'

All the while, he was frantically trying to figure out what had happened to them and what exactly this strange "Twilk" creature standing in front of them was!?

The Twilk, realising he had spoken a little too sharply and hoping to calm the children a little, changed its tone and began to speak more gently. Clearing its throat, it softly spoke.

'Ahem... I am sorry for my bad manners,' it said, 'I will start at the beginning. My name is Tag and I am an elder Twilk!' he went on... 'It appears that you have entered the magical Land of Sreen!'

'Where?' both children questioned, 'the magical land of where?' they repeated, as they had not heard the name before. They both gasped, 'Magical!?' as they were stunned at the thought of magic being real!...

'The Land of Sreen,' repeated Tag. 'In fact, you are in the Province of Umble Down,' he declared, gesturing behind them with his hand. 'That is Umble Down Castle!' he said proudly.

As the children spun around to look, they couldn't believe their eyes. It was truly fantastic. Beyond the feathery grass, through a hazy mist, rose a group of hills standing alone, but proudly and strongly. Two beautiful, shimmering, fairy-tale towers stood glistening in the sunlight at the top of the largest hill. Umble Down Castle was perfectly placed for overseeing the Province of Umble Down.

'The colours are amazing, like shiny seashells,' said Elvie, bewitched by its beauty.

Although fantastic, it was too much for them to understand, and both children held each other's arms for support. Tag could see how bewildered the children were, and by now was feeling very sorry for them. He gestured for them to sit down in front of a bale of Feather Fuzzy and said calmly.

'Sit here and try to relax, I will pop into my house and get a map to show you where you are.' With that he walked off and entered the knobbly rustic wooden house opposite the bale of Feather Fuzzy.

'Do you think we're dreaming?' asked Aiden.

'Not sure!' Elvie replied, sounding a little shaky.

'Let's eat the rest of our lunch. It might make us feel a little bit better.' Aiden said hopefully.

So the children took the food from their bags, and went about eating something, whilst trying to take in the extraordinary scenery around them.

'This pork pie is great,' mumbled Aiden with his mouth full.

'I don't seem to be able to eat a thing.' Elvie sat with a worried look on her face and feeling quite anxious.

'Here it is,' shouted Tag excitedly, as he reappeared from his house, waving the map in front of them.

Elvie, shedding a small tear, said as politely as she could. 'Thank you Tag, but does it show us the way home?'

'Oh my dear,' said Tag kindly at seeing her distress, 'I can take you home, for I am the magic keeper,' he said proudly. 'I have the magical power to transport you back to your realm. We can go now if you like?'

'Yes that would be great,' said Elvie, relieved, thinking just how weird it sounded, being in another "realm"!!... Tag gestured impatiently with his hands for the children to stand up, then, stubbornly pressed the map into Aiden's hands.

'Please take this', he said urgently, 'it's magical, and will show you all you need to know about the Land of Sreen and Umble Down.'

'But why do we need it if you are taking us home?' asked Aiden bewildered.

Tag calmly and quietly explained, 'The fact that you are here means the magic of Sreen is fading. Soon, we will no longer be able to keep ourselves hidden from your world,' he added frankly, 'furthermore, it is written in the old books of Sreen, that the first humans seen by a Twilk will be destined to save our world, but if more come, they will be scared – They will fear us and try to destroy us.' He continued encouragingly, 'You have been drawn to Sreen and to me by magic itself. Your destinies are to do good and save our homeland.' He went on, 'I trust you both, and even though this is sudden for you, I have been expecting this day for some time now. It is your destiny that you found Sreen, and I hope you can both rise to the challenges that lay ahead of you!'

The children looked quite perplexed.

'Challenges ahead of us? What are you saying?' said Aiden, feeling angry that someone dared to give him a challenge. After all, he was supposed to be relaxing and enjoying the summer holidays!

Tag tried to reassure him. 'I hope you can forgive me for being stern when we first met?' he asked softly, with a worried gaze, 'please, trust me, we need you to save the magic!'

It was a shocking thing to hear and the children felt quite overwhelmed. Tag raised his hand, about to click his fingers and paused, 'One more thing; the map must stay safe with you! It is magically woven now, to you and to the soul of Sreen. If it ever gets into the wrong hands it might destroy both of our worlds – forever!...

With that, Tag clicked his fingers. The children felt a sudden warm breeze touch their cheeks, their ears tingled as a buzzing and whooshing sound reverberated in their heads. All of a sudden, they found themselves back home in the woods near their den. The words of Tag were running through their heads.

'It's all in the map!'

* * *

Dizzily, but in silence, they looked at each other sitting crossed legged on the woodland floor amongst the damp leaves and twigs. After getting their breath back and still a little shocked, they finally spoke.

'Did that really happen?' asked Elvie, frowning with confusion.

'The fact that I know what you are talking about, and I have the map in my hands, means that it did!' Aiden was without doubt. He began to hurry, 'We must pull ourselves together so that we can explain to Mum why we are late.' Putting the map in his bag and looking at his watch, he added with surprise, 'that's odd, we've only been gone for two minutes, but it feels like we have been gone for over an hour!'

'Time must go quicker there!' added Elvie, feeling very happy to be home.

Excitedly, and somewhat in disbelief, the children chatted about their amazing adventure. They agreed not to tell their mum and dad about it for now, but also shook hands on telling if they felt they were in any danger.

'They wouldn't believe us anyway!' Elvie giggled. With that, the children made their way home, dusting each other off to remove any feathery evidence.

'Meet me in my bedroom tonight, and we'll look at the map.' Aiden commanded.

'Yes Sir!' saluted Elvie, 'after tea,' she giggled again.

For the rest of the day they quietly avoided each other. So many thoughts and questions raced through their young heads. To distract herself Elvie calmly helped their mum with the house work and Aiden absentmindedly stared at a book, trying to read. Secretly inside though, they were extremely excited and full of trepidation about what adventures might lay ahead of them!

Chapter 3

A Magical Map

Knock! Knock! Elvie stood outside Aiden's bedroom waiting in anticipation to be let in. She felt a knot of excitement growing in her tummy.

'Come in – phew, I'm glad it's only you,' he said, not wishing to be found out. 'I thought it might be Mum!'

It was seven o'clock in the evening and the Baldwins had just finished their dinner.

'I panicked because I suddenly thought we'd lost the map.' Elvie blurted out with confusion, looking for her brother's support as she walked in.

'It's OK, I've hidden it safely away,' he said smugly, 'but you're not to see where I get it from, that way you won't be able to slip up and tell anyone else where it is.'

'Good idea,' agreed Elvie. She turned away, closing her eyes and covering her ears. Secretly she was quite relieved, but also mildly surprised that she wasn't feeling a bit jealous that Aiden had taken control of the map.

Aiden's room was just about big enough to hold his bed, wardrobe, chest of draws, and bookshelves. There was a square of space at the foot of his bed in front of his window to lay around on, if needed. Clearing a space on the floor amongst his books, they laid the map down in the centre. It was a square, thick wodge of folded layers, old but not flaky, and whiter than you would expect, with feathery stuff pressed into its fibres. There were no tears or marks, just a wavy edged flap from the bottom right corner to the top left.

'OPEN IT!' urged Elvie excitedly. Aiden's fingers hesitantly reached for the top left corner of the flap to open it (treating it like the pages of a precious book), but before he was able to, the map began frantically spinning on the floor. Gasping, both children jumped backwards in surprise. A good job too, because the map unfurled itself in front of them, covering most of the floor area at the foot of the bed.

'That nearly went in my eye!' Aiden frowned angrily, as he realised he had ended up inside his wardrobe, which had fortunately been left open! Looking at Elvie, he could see she had managed to jump onto the bed, her knees tucked under her chin as she hugged her legs.

'WOW, obviously doesn't matter which way up it is!' she said.

Thinking about it, Aiden realised what was going on and tried his best to explain. 'It seems to open if we want it to, like it knows when it's needed!'

There in front of them laid the map. From where he was crouching in front of the wardrobe, Aiden could clearly see the title of the map. Elvie had to lie over the bed, and turn her head to the right, but could see it read in bold, 'The Land of Sreen' and was written in an odd, blue ink, with a purplish tinge. The paper was rough and lumpy, with feathers and black bits, like the paper they had made at home with their mum. Quickly, they glanced over the map scanning it at speed. They couldn't really take it all in. There was so much to see.

'AWESOME!' Aiden exclaimed loudly!

'You bet.' Elvie replied as she moved awkwardly from the bed to her brothers' side to get a closer look at the map.

'Wow, it's amazing!' she tried to keep her voice to a whisper, worried that their mum may hear them.

Underneath the title, the map was skilfully drawn in the same colour ink. It was clearly divided into three areas called Provinces. These were named – Umble Up, Umble Down, and Umble Over. It gave, in some detail, places and areas of importance. The mountains, the rivers, High Mill, Umble Down Castle, woodlands, fields, lakes, crops and flowers, pathways and houses. Oddly, the children noticed that Umble Down castle was at the top of a hill, Umble Up was at the bottom of a crater, and

Umble Over was reached by a pass which ran through the middle of a mountain!

'So this is Sreen!' stated Aiden, in a very matter of fact way.

'Looks like it,' replied Elvie thoughtfully, 'that field is labelled "Feather Fuzzy", which must be where all those bales of feathers were that we landed on this morning. So that is where we were!' she added proudly, now she was getting her bearings.

'I'm not sure how this map can help us?' wondered Aiden. Suddenly, as if in reply to his doubts, the map began to shimmer. Different colours began to mix and swirl in front of their eyes, as the map transformed into what could only be described as a vision!

'It's in 3D now!' remarked Elvie.

'More like it's alive!' replied Aiden nervously.

They were both, once again, shocked and worried about what may happen next when they heard a soothing voice speak out to them and give some directions.

"The colourful land of Sreen is easy to navigate."

'Was that in our heads or was it out loud?' asked Aiden.

'I'm not actually sure?' replied Elvie, feeling quite confused, 'but I've heard it before. I think – no, – I *know*, its Tag's voice.' She said.

Looking back at the map, there was now a scene playing out in front of them, like looking at a floating holographic TV screen. They could easily identify Umble Down, where they had met Tag. His voice was calmly and quietly guiding them around the rest of the map. He explained that they were looking at bales of Feather Fuzzy, which is grown at the foot of Middle Big Hill, where Umble Down Castle stood proudly at the top. There were two smaller hills on either side that rolled gently down to the Feather Fuzzy, but these had no names. Houses that looked like wooden huts were dotted all around. The colours of the landscape were very vivid! The Feather Fuzzy seemed to cloud the hills in a dense, white fog of fluff, which contrasted with the lively green of the grass and the vibrant meadow flowers growing in the meadows beyond the crop fields.

The children looked on silently as they were shown the dark and eerie Grickle Woods, where only a few brave Twilk go to harvest and gather the gnarled and spiky Grickle wood! It had a wonderful mix of tones to its trunks and branches, ranging from pale oatmeal to dark ebony! The thorns, being sharper than any knife, were sought after to make tools and the occasional weapon.

'Look at how brightly coloured the flowers are, they look like they have been painted!' remarked Elvie.

'Not only that, but they are such odd shapes.' Aiden added, as he noticed the hearts, swirls and zig-zags.

'I'm feeling a little travel sick now,' moaned Elvie.

The map's action made them feel like they were now flying around a three-dimensional Sreen at a very fast pace. Tag's voice had stopped altogether now as they started going much faster.

The trees and view swept past, quicker and quicker. A rainbow coloured lake, a strange tall mill with two sets of sails, one above the other. Faster, faster, a river, a bridge, a farm, faster, faster, strange sheep, cows and horses, even dogs were swept past their vision in a blur as the map raced over the bizarre land they gazed upon below.

'STOP!' yelled Aiden, 'it's going too fast,' he jumped angrily to his feet. 'I can't remember any of it,' he said irritably.

Maybe you won't have to remember!' added Elvie thoughtfully.

'What do you mean Elvie?' asked Aiden, raising his eyebrows.

'I mean, it feels to me like I know the place, like I have somehow soaked it all in.' she replied, eyes wide with wonderment.

Aiden took a deep breath and thought about what Elvie had said.

'Oh yes, me too now,' he smiled cheerfully to himself, suddenly aware and at ease with his new found information, 'it's like it's my home,' he said.

Being so engrossed in their newly acquired knowledge, neither child noticed the map fold itself up and settle, as it had begun, as a square of old folded paper on the floor.

Excitedly they spoke to each other. 'Did you see those clouds?' asked Aiden.

'They were pale pink.' Elvie shouted eagerly.

'And the sheep!' exclaimed Aiden, 'they were all different colours!' He grabbed his head in disbelief.

At that moment, their mum came into Aiden's room. 'What are different colours?' she asked softly.

'Oh nothing, we were only making up stories.' replied Elvie calmly, and thinking quickly to throw her mum off the scent.

'OK then,' she said, 'supper in two minutes.' She left the room, calling out cheerfully, 'and be sure to throw that paper in your bin before you come downstairs!'

'Phew that was close!' Elvie gasped.

'Yes, we'll have to be much more careful next time!' agreed Aiden. They both knew that any messy bits of paper their mum found laying around would normally end up in the paper shredder! Following their mums exit from the room, Aiden discreetly hid the map safely away without Elvie seeing. 'Let's have supper' he said with a sigh, he was now feeling drained from the nervous excitement.

By now, exhausted and still quite bemused by the odd and bizarre events of the day, they both went downstairs to see what was for supper. Milk and biscuits, that was good news as far as the children were concerned and they slowly enjoyed them before wearily going to bed.

Chapter 4

Legend of the Dragon Gem

The next morning, the children awoke from a very deep sleep. They were too excited to be tired, but were ravenously hungry. They quickly polished off cereals, toast, and fruit for their breakfast, while sitting at the old pine kitchen table.

While their mum was busying herself in the kitchen, both children were making up a plan for the day ahead – in code!

'Today, I would like to go back to the woods and finish off our den!' chirped Elvie.

'Good idea!' Aiden managed to sound normal. He realised that he would usually refuse to go anywhere with his sister, just for the sake of winding her up, so he added 'maybe!' to sound less eager, but it didn't work.

Spinning around, their mum said teasingly, 'So what's all this about then? You two happily doing something together!? Whatever next?' she carried on, amusing herself, 'maybe you'll tidy your rooms without being asked?!'

'Now hang on!' laughed Aiden, trying to act naturally.

'Well anyway, I'll get you some lunch to take with you,' she said turning away 'I like it when you're playing nicely together, it makes me happy!' she added cheerfully.

'That was close again,' Elvie mouthed to Aiden. Then she spoke out loud in an obvious way, so that her mum would hear her, but using code so that only Aiden knew what she meant. 'I'll get washed and dressed first, then, when you have got your bag packed, it'll be your turn.' She motioned her eyes upwards and flicked her head in the direction of Aiden's room. He knew that she was telling him to remember to pack the map in his bag before they left the house.

'OK, will do,' he answered happily, then added more sternly 'when I'm ready.' He hoped that his mum wouldn't notice his unusually helpful mood.

Twenty minutes later, they were walking, with bags on their backs, across the playing field towards the woods. The weather was much nicer than the day before, as if the sun had come out to help them! Excited about life, they began to race each other towards the edge of the woods.

'I won!' Aiden shouted full of pride, but then he promptly tripped and fell into the undergrowth.

'Serves you right!' said Elvie unsympathetically. 'You always boast like that when you win, but what do you expect? You're older and bigger than me!' she added righteously. Just then, Elvie heard a loud rustling in the woods behind them. Both children turned to see some of the undergrowth flapping, as if moved by someone walking past. They slowly stood up and carefully walked towards the patch of greenery. Looking at each other nervously, they were, by now, prepared for almost anything.

There was a sudden 'CRACK'. They both jumped back as a rabbit scurried past their feet, ran along the edge of the field and back into some brambles at the far end of the woods.

'I don't know what I was expecting?' laughed Elvie, surprised and relieved.

'Phew!' Aiden Giggled, 'we're not very intrepid, are we?' They both decided to carry on to the Den and try to work out what was going to happen next. Suddenly, from out of the branches above them, a twig fell and landed directly at their feet. Looking up to see where it had come from, they saw Tag sitting on a low branch. He was dangling his long legs over the edge and swinging them backwards and forwards. 'Are you supposed to be here?' asked Elvie with genuine concern, 'what if you are seen?' Tag turned sideways and virtually disappeared.

'Good camouflage!' Aiden pointed out.

'OK, Point taken.' said Elvie sheepishly.

Neither child had noticed that Tag had stealthily climbed down from the tree. As if to prove a point, he quietly walked around them and suddenly appeared in front of them.

'Ready?' Tag spoke calmly, and quietly. Elvie jumped back in surprise when she looked down to see Tag at her feet. Aiden was in awe of his ability to conceal himself so easily.

'Are we to come with you now Tag?' Elvie queried, still feeling shocked and somewhat unprepared.

Smiling and eager for adventure, Aiden answered impulsively, 'As I'll ever be.'

Elvie, not wanting to leave her brothers side, answered inconfidently, 'All systems go then!' She was wondering how wise they had been to carry on with this adventure, and hoped she sounded tougher than she was feeling. Seeing the doubt in her face, Aiden put his arm around her to comfort her.

'It's OK Elvie, remember, we already know Sreen now, in our minds!' he said softly.

'I know!' she answered, 'but the Twilks don't know us!' she exclaimed.

'All will be well.' Tag intervened calmly again, and without giving her any time to answer or even think about it, he lifted up his arm and clicked his fingers. As before, they felt the air brush their faces, and a tingling spread all over their bodies. With a firm whoosh, they were carried magically back to the land they now knew of as Sreen.

'Probably will never really be able to get used to that!' remarked Aiden, as he stumbled and found his feet.

'I know what you mean.' Elvie replied, feeling a little bit wobbly and slightly woozy.

'IT BEGINS!' declared Tag seriously.

'By that I hope you mean our mission?' said Aiden, who by now, was really getting into the spirit of the adventures that lay ahead!

* * *

They had landed at the foot of what they knew to be Umble Down Castle. The towering walls shimmered intensely with rainbow colours in the bright sunlight. Standing beside the glistening walls of the castle on top of Middle Big Hill, the children looked out over the Province of Umble Down.

'Stunning!' remarked Aiden.

'Beautiful!' Elvie added.

They could see all they had learned from the map, and remembered in great detail much about the place; like how years ago, many of the houses in Sreen had been made from Blast Sandstone. This was mined at Topple End, to the south of the province of Umble Down. It was mined for its beauty. Every surface glittered like Mother of Pearl, pink, yellow, blue, green, purple. How, over time, Twilks had begun to use Grickle wood to build their homes because it was easier to move, and quicker to build with, plus it grew back quickly to replenish itself. How the mine, which was more like a large pit, became disused and eventually, over the years, filled with rainwater. The lake now glistens there, reflecting the blast sandstone bottom, like precious gems and rainbow dust.

The landscape shone at them. Bright and lively green fields marked the plateau beyond the swaying fields of Feather Fuzzy. Strange Yooze, Mooze, and Nimble Leg Carriers grazed among the rich and striking colours of the meadow flowers. Twilks worked their crops in the fields under the sunny skies. The fragrance on the air was sweet and fresh.

'As splendid as the land of Sreen is, I must remind you that you still have a job to do!' Tag gestured with his hand, as he pointed to what looked like a break in the sky. It looked as if the air had a hole in it.

'It looks like a piece of melted cling film!' remarked Elvie.

'That's the magic failing!' replied Tag sadly. 'We have three layers around us, and *that* is the first layer dissolving,' he explained anxiously.

'Why can't you just make more magic?' Aiden asked seriously.

'We are unable to.' replied Tag. 'Since the Great Dragon War, 250 Twilk years ago, it has been forbidden. All because a greedy Twilk named Ilex misused his magic.'

'Who forbi..forbided..forb..forbade it?' asked Aiden, grinning at his sister to make her think he'd said it wrongly on purpose, but still unsure he'd picked the right word!?

'King Neema and Queen Amari – The King and Queen of Sreen!' he said 'since then, young Twilks have not been taught to use magic, and so cannot perform it.' He added sadly.

'But you can?!' Elvie said suspiciously.

'Yes, a few elders and I, but that's all. We are not strong enough to mend a tear in magic itself, the force would kill us!' he said sadly hanging his head. 'We need the power of the diamond to help!'

'DIAMOND!?' both children answered excitedly in unison.

'Yes, the "Mirror Diamond", it absorbs energy from around it then reflects it back out, allowing it's keeper to use the energy.'

'Wow, that sounds impressive,' said Aiden in wonderment.

Elvie still wanted to find out more about Tag. 'You must be a couple of hundred years old then if you can still use magic?' she questioned almost in disbelief.

'I am indeed, and I was there in the War' he stood straight and proud.

'Wow!' said Aiden in awe 'Are the King and Queen still alive then?'

'Yes,' replied Tag haplessly, 'they live in safety at Umble Down Castle and shall remain there until the threat is over – or until the end!'

'Tell us more about the war?' asked Elvie.

Tag obliged. 'It was a time of great ease and happiness, when all Twilk made magic. A time of the old ones!' he said reminiscing, 'things were easy and free. Magic was made from thoughts. As children, we learned to think happily and carefully. We put greed aside and used positive magical thinking to create a safe and good place, with a bounty of wonderful things.' He added with some seriousness, 'Furthermore, we were taught only to use the magic for the good of all,' Aiden and Elvie were smiling at the unusual tales as Tag continued with his story. 'It was the time of the dragons, when we Twilk lived happily alongside the beasts. Both sides had magic and power, and both sides respected each other. The dragons lived quietly in the mountains, while we Twilk lived everywhere else. Our magic was so powerful that even the fairy folk befriended us, knowing they could not affect us with their mischievous ways.' Tag added proudly, 'Even now, they still leave us alone!'

'Huh – it just had to be *dragons and fairies*!' said Aiden scornfully.

'There really *are* fairies?!' Elvie exclaimed, trying to contain her sudden excitement at the prospect of actually meeting one!

Tag looked at Elvie with a raised eyebrow as if to say, 'Do you really need to ask?' he continued, 'Since time began, the Dragons had their own way of making magic. Nobody knew how, but they were truly magical – and breath-taking too. All Twilks admired and respected them, that is, until the antics of a greedy young Twilk called Ilex.' With a deep sigh, he continued, 'He hadn't been taught well, and didn't understand the enormity of the power of magic, or the consequences of any action that may not be for the good of all. He wanted to be powerful and mighty, and so, one day he chose to spy on the Dragons in an attempt to gain valuable knowledge of their magic.'

Both children were listening intently by now. 'Taking his life in his hands, he secretly followed them, watching them wherever they went – day in and day out – always hidden. As he watched, he discovered that all the dragons frequently visited a large cave in the mountains. This mountain no longer exists. It is just a large Crater in the ground at Umble Up!' Tag's face looked sad.

'Why is there not a mountain anymore?' asked Aiden.

'I don't think I'm going to like this!' Elvie added nervously.

'One day,' Tag continued, 'Ilex used all of his ability to silently and stealthily creep into the cave unseen and unheard. He discovered, at the foot of a pile of rocks, an enormous diamond, the size of one of your footballs.'

'Wow,' both children replied, again in unison, '"Mirror Diamond"!'

'It, of course, was the reason the Dragons magic was so powerful. Anyone standing near it could feel the power radiating from it, or so we're told.' Tag added. 'Eventually the temptation of power had beguiled Ilex. After much underhanded and roguish cunning, he was able to steal the stone from the dragons' lair. Once in possession of the magical rock, and because it was *so* powerful, Ilex's thinking became twisted, as the diamond powerfully reflected his badness back to him. The true power of magic created his downfall. He imagined such bad things, which to his delight, happened instantly.' Tag continued 'The dragons were shocked and traumatised. They waged war on Sreen and on all Twilks for stealing their diamond gem. Ilex was feared by all, as he tried to rule the Provinces and the dragons with his evil power. However, he met his downfall as his evil mind trapped him. He began to hate being alone, and then he hated himself for his miserable life and wished he was dead. That's exactly what happened; He died from his own magical wish!..'

'Why did the war continue?' asked Elvie.

'Twilks tried to make peace with the dragons,' he said, 'but were thwarted by the angriest dragon families who believed that we still had the diamond – we did not!

Eventually, the dragons, after destroying our homes and land searching for the rock, began to fight each other. Those who wanted revenge, against those who wanted to make peace and forgive. The very last remaining dragons fought a fierce and savage battle at the top of the mountain. Their fire was so fierce, not only did they destroy themselves but they also annihilated the top of the mountain – leaving only a crater!' He sounded exhausted.

'Umble Up!' exclaimed Elvie, remembering the map.

'Our job is to find the diamond I take it?' asked Aiden courageously.

'That will be a lot easier without dragons!' Elvie laughed with relief.

Tag wistfully continued, 'The land stayed barren for many years until eventually, plants started to grow back and a few animals made it their home. A stream made its way through the rocks. As time went on, the Twilk forgot about the dragons and built their homes in the crater. Umble Up is now a beautiful place and the stream glistens with golden hues. Umble Down castle was also rebuilt, along with High Mill on the river Tong!'

He added for interest. 'It is all beautiful now, but without the dragon's "Mirror Diamond", we will not be able to mend the magic, and Sreen and the Twilks will disappear forever!' he exclaimed.

'We must hurry,' urged Aiden, readying himself for the journey.

'You will not be seen by Twilks,' said Tag helpfully, 'I have veiled you with magic. Try not to get too close, as they may sense your presence and become alarmed.' he added thoughtfully. 'One more thing, time moves more slowly here. If you spend a night in Sreen, only an hour or so will have passed in your world.' With that, he disappeared and the children heard his distant voice call,

'Time is running out!...'

Chapter 5

They Ramble to Umble Up

Standing alone, at the foot of Umble Down Castle, both children took a deep breath in, ready to start their journey.

'I don't understand why it's up to us to find this "Mirror Diamond"?' quizzed Elvie.

'I'm not sure either, but Tag said it's because the magic needed us!' Aiden sounded doubtful. 'What's so special about us?' he thought.

'Let's forget about that for now, and get on with the task in hand.' Elvie said, being as organised as ever. 'The sooner we find it the better for all of us.' She added impatiently.

'I vote we go to...' before Aiden could finish his sentence, Elvie cheekily jumped in with;

'Umble Up!'

'Lucky for you sis, that's exactly what I was going to say!' He patiently put his arm around Elvie's shoulders and gave her an affectionate squeeze. They got the map out and it unfurled in their hands. It opened into a square that showed them the route to Umble Up.

'This looks quite easy!' stated Elvie happily as they began walking along the path in front of them. They were going down Middle Big Hill heading towards Feather Fuzzy Fields.

'Look!' said Aiden, 'I believe we need to head towards High Mill,' he indicated ahead into the distance. 'You can see the path from here.' He pointed it out.

'It's so beautiful here!' remarked Elvie as she took in the view, 'the air is so sweet and balmy and the clouds are the colour of the flowers,' she added dreamily.

'Be that as it may,' said Aiden 'we still need to get a move on.' He motioned his head towards the sky. The tear in the magic was getting larger. Looking at it, they both noticed some strange, dark grey birds flying by, and circling as if to linger and watch them. Both children shuddered at the presence of the birds, but continued on their journey. Aiden felt they looked like trouble and made a mental note to keep his eye on them.

The children started their ramble quite quickly, passing the fields of swaying Feather Fuzzy, with its heady perfume (like candy floss roses), and wondered how anyone got any work done! Relaxing more into the journey they decided to swap stories of their magical visions and new found memories.

'OK, let's recap and compare our new thoughts to make sure that they match before we do anything else.' Aiden suggested.

'Good idea!' replied Elvie, 'that way I may be able to help you understand a bit more!' she said, cheekily nudging her brother with her elbow. 'You go first Aiden'

'I'll start with the animals!' he announced and then began recounting his new knowledge.

'Yooze, it's a type of sheep, which has various bright colours in its fleece. Like our sheep at home, they are used to produce wool, but unlike home, no dyeing is required due to the original colours of the fleece. Which explains Tag's clothing choice – a bit too bright if you ask me?!' He grinned impishly. 'The meat is apparently quite delicious, and they are good for cutting the grass too.'

'Check!' affirmed Elvie.

'Mooze,' he went on, 'is a type of cow, they look similar to ours only smaller and thinner, but they produce milk which is flavoured by the magical flowers they eat.'

'Check'. Elvie stared at him with her intense eyes, waiting for the next animal. They both stopped and sat down resting a while on the grass, the morning sun warming their backs.

'Woofnsnappers are small dogs.' he added quickly.

'Check! more, more' Elvie was impatient to move on.

'Nimble Leg Carriers are a type of horse, with very long legs and slim bodies. Stronger than they look, and extremely fast,' he added.

'Yes, yes, my turn!' Elvie jumped ahead of him on the path. 'I remember that the Harmony butterfly only lives at Umble Over, and is also very colourful. Its colours change like a chameleon, but with every beat of its wings. Not only that, but the beating wings make beautiful sounds – like crystal chimes and angelic music.'

'Check!' Aiden copied Elvie's lead.

'Dreep flour,' she said 'is made from Dreep grain, grown at Topple End Farm by the Trickle family. They lived in one of the last remaining Blast sandstone houses – other than the Castle!'

'Yes,' replied Aiden 'and it is blue because of the mineral Blast, which is only found in the soil at Topple End.'

'Correct!' stated Elvie.

'Blue Tan is an alcohol made from Dreep grain husks, sugar and water,' he added 'It is deep blue in colour because of the Blast mineral taken up by the Dreep plants, and it's only for adults as it can be very strong!'

The memory recap had turned more into a game than in any preparation for their adventure.

By now, they had reached High Mill with its double set of sails, so they stopped to have a brief rest. They sat down in front of a group of bushes that surrounded the clearing of the mill. They were trying to be discrete, as Tag had told them. They saw at least thirty Twilk working hard at the Mill. They were all wearing a type of overall that had clearly been made from (very bright) yellow Yooze wool, and were dusty with blue floury finger marks. The mill was very tall and imposing, with two huge sets of indigo blue sails made from Dreep jute.

'I know that Tag said be careful not to be noticed, but this is too interesting to be missed!' With that Aiden had darted off inside the mill. He could never miss out on anything technical! Elvie, not feeling quite so intrepid, stayed on her spot, wishing that Aiden was not such a *boy*!!

While inside the mill, Aiden was amazed at its height. It seemed large even for a human! There were four floors with a huge grinding stone on each level and reached by a central spiral staircase. The two sets of sails turned the stones, which in turn, ground the grain. It went like clockwork. After the first grinding, the grain husks were separated in large sieves on the top floor and bagged up for Nimble Leg feed. The Dreep grain needed to be ground four times to make it soft enough for Twilks to use in cooking. It was passed from one grinding stone through wooden chutes to the next. The bottom stone ground the finest flour of all. Having seen enough, Aiden quickly darted back to where he had left Elvie, who was by now feeling quite relaxed.

She announced. 'Do you realise these Twilks really can't see us!' she sounded amazed!

'I'm not sure that they care!' remarked Aiden.

'They all seem to be half asleep to me.'

'You're quite right!' Elvie agreed, 'they all look like they're in a dream.'

She brushed his shoulder to remove a patch of blue dusty flour from his clothing. Aiden felt uncomfortable and quite worried. 'Things were starting to not add up properly!' he thought to himself.

They pushed on with their trek, over the River Tong via Mill Bridge. The water looked clear and fresh. River weeds clung to rocks, anchored by their roots, and floating in drifts in the direction of the current.

Aiden, trying to be light hearted said 'It's just like any river back home, I thought we would see Purple Snouted Umbrella Fish!' and he laughed almost awkwardly.

'Very funny,' answered Elvie wryly, then she pointed out, 'not everything is different here, some of the trees and grasses are the same as home.'

The mood had definitely improved.

Moving on, they headed towards the Sweet Dew Bush thicket, indicated on the map. The terrain had changed, and they were now walking on sandy and rocky heathland, which was studded with prickly gorse bushes and heathers.

While they walked, Aiden noticed more strange grey birds fly past, as if they were following them. He hoped Elvie hadn't seen them. He chose to say nothing, and just tried to ignore them. He also chose not to mention the complete lack of Twilk anywhere!?

They came across a large area of short grass with what looked like evidence of recent rabbit activity!

'LOOK!' Elvie shouted happily, 'Sweet Dew Bushes!'

She was delighted by them, with their triangular dark greeny blue leaves, thornless stems and large knobbly bright red fruits, which reminded her of raspberries, but were firm and bouncy when picked.

'They smell like marshmallows.' Aiden noted hungrily.

'Yes, let's try one.' Elvie replied. She would normally be much more careful about eating anything wild, but her new memories somehow told her it was reasonably safe, as these were a regular fruit. They were also, however, a relaxant and sedative, so she knew not to eat lots!

'Ok, but only one remember, or they will make us drowsy!' Aiden said sternly. Elvie took one and ate it. The flavour danced around her tongue, like an explosion of colours in a prism.

'So refreshing, like all fruits and flowers, yet relaxing like music!' she proclaimed.

Aiden had also eaten one. 'It tastes of summer and happiness!' he said feeling quite serene.

Refreshed from their snack, and still picking the pips from their teeth, they moved on with their journey. Quietly, Elvie put some of the already picked berries in her pocket, just in case they got peckish later on in the day!

A stony, gravel path now led them past a few grickle wood houses to their left, and Rainbow Lake, to their right. The houses looked strong and beautiful. They were mottled in a variety of tones by the shade of the wood grain, its knots and age. Older wood was dark – almost ebony black. Younger wood was a pale yellow – almost white. Every piece was a different shade. Every house was built in a different shape to the next. Pale sun-bleached Dreep straw thatched the roofs completing the rustic look with a knobbly, tufty, mop-head top to each home. It was strange to the children that the Twilk's houses were so small – like 'Wendy houses', they thought.

As they quietly chatted their way past the silent houses, another grey bird perched on one of the roofs. Ignoring it, Aiden turned to Elvie and said.

'You remember that those berries are made into Slumber Cup liquor?,' without giving her any chance to answer, he added, 'do you think somehow, the Twilk have all been given some, and that's why they look half asleep?'

'But why would they drink it knowingly?' replied Elvie.

'That's what is puzzling me!' said Aiden.

'Hold that thought!' said Elvie hastily pointing ahead. They had arrived at their destination. Umble Up! They stood side by side at the top edge of an enormous circular crater, which was concealed by its size and by the natural undergrowth and shrubbery.

'It's so large, I almost missed it!' remarked Aiden. Surveying the view, Elvie noticed at the bottom of the crater some more houses and a river. She pointed out a path which led down the sides of the crater to the houses.

'There's no time like the present,' Aiden said, as he carefully started down the pathway, 'be careful it is very slippery and steep!' he said.

The path was sandy and gravelly. Placing their feet carefully the children clambered down grabbing bushes and trees. Loose gravel skidded underfoot and tufts of grass helped keep their footing. Mini landslides trickled down the crater as the children slowly and silently made their way down the zigzag path. The breeze cooled their hot faces, while their hands stayed warm, but dusty, from their efforts. The colour of the sky changed from the reflection of the meadow flowers at Umble Down, to the green of the grass and bushes at Umble Up!

'You OK?' Aiden asked, as he reached the bottom first. Huffing and puffing, Elvie finally got her feet on the level ground.

'Phew, yes. It's just that I'm hot.' Elvie replied, very relieved to be at the bottom. 'I need a drink now,' she got her water from her backpack.

A screech sounded above them in the sky, as a single grey bird circled over them and then flew off, back in the direction from where they had come. The children sat on the ground, with their elbows leaning on bended knees, heads lowered, taking a rest. It was eerily quiet, and both children, although not mentioning it to each other, felt that something was wrong.

'Not far to go now!' Aiden said with encouragement, pointing through the woods that lay ahead.

'Yes, so let's get going or we will be here all day!' Elvie replied. The eeriness made her feel like hurrying away from there. Secretly, all she wanted to do was to go home.

Chapter 6

Calling the Dragon

Umble Up was a small grickle wood village nestled amongst the trees.

'It's quiet, quaint and beautiful!' Said Elvie, as they came out of the woodland and arrived at the village.

'Shh, someone might hear us.' Aiden urged.

The village Twilks were busying themselves with everyday tasks. They were exercising woofnsnappers, mending their houses, tending to the crops in the fields, and hanging out their clothes. But they all appeared to be in a dream. Not one Twilk noticed the children, or even looked around at each other!

Elvie wondered, 'Why are they all so dozy, just like they were at the mill?'

'Listen!' Aiden pointed towards the river, where he could hear the distant sound of voices. Cautiously, they approached the sandy banks and hid behind a suitably large enough bush. Looking through the leaves they could see young Twilks, slowly playing in the river, and lazily trying to lift something out.

'Quick, you try!' said one of them, their voices high pitched, as with all young Twilk.

Aiden and Elvie could see through the clear river water from their vantage point. The river bed was gravelly, with large areas of rocks and pebbles. It was at one such area that a few of the Twilks were unsuccessfully, and quite lethargically, grasping at something on the river bottom. Reaching and grabbing, snatching and grappling. Whatever it was, no sooner did they touch it, than it escaped their grasp! After quite some time, the young Twilks gave up and wandered off. Aiden and Elvie, needing to stretch, moved out of their hiding place for a closer look.

Now that the river was free of Twilks, they could see a golden, leaf shaped object, nestled on the bottom of the river bed. Moving closer, and standing on the very edge of the sandy river bank, the children could now see a cluster of these large, yellow metallic leaf shaped objects, glistening and sparkling like gold in the gravel.

'What do you think they are?' asked Elvie.

'Well they're *not* the diamond, are they?' replied Aiden turning to look at his sister. He was about to suggest that they may be fossils, when to his surprise, Elvie was already ankle deep in the river, trying to keep her balance on the stones.

'WHAT ARE YOU DOING?' he shouted in alarm.

'I think they're important!' she replied, but as she looked up, she stumbled, lost her footing, and plunged headlong into the deepest part of the river.

Aiden Gasped. 'ARE YOU OK?' he shouted across to Elvie, frightened by his sister's impulsiveness.

'I'm fine, actually it's quite cooling!' she replied unconcerned. 'But guess what?' she beamed excitedly and giggled, 'I've got one!'

'No, you can't have, that's ridiculous. Those Twilks have been trying for ages!' He said, surprised and quite perplexed. Little did either of them know, but the young Twilk had been trying to achieve this feat unsuccessfully all their lifetime! This was to prove quite an important event for everybody!!..

Elvie clambered onto the river bank, all wet and bedraggled, but triumphantly clutching her prize. Aiden got the map out to hopefully find some sort of information about these strange and wonderful golden objects.

'Wow, it is *so* sparkly.' Elvie said, holding it up to admire it. The curious object shimmered and glistened in the light. Elvie found the thing strangely lightweight, but extremely strong as she examined it more thoroughly.

'Yes, there's a reason for that,' said Aiden, irritated and more than a little anxious. 'The map informs me that this is Dragon River, and I quote – "It is a myth that dragon scales have laid here since the dragon wars.

Never have they been removed and can only be removed by a pure seeker of truth!"' He said abruptly.

'Oops,' replied Elvie, 'that must be me then?' she said giggling naively, unsure of her words and wrinkling her top lip.

'Yes.' replied Aiden, looking uneasy and with a patronising tone. 'What's more, the myth also tells us that whoever removes the dragon scale from the river, automatically calls the dragon!

'Oh dear,' Elvie winced, 'anyway, the legend also says that the dragons destroyed each other years ago, so they can't be called any more – *can they!*!' she said bolshily, hoping to cover up her fear.

'I've got a feeling that we will find out *now*, won't we!' replied Aiden assertively. He was a little annoyed at Elvie's actions, and fearing the consequences.

They heard another screech from above and looked up to see a collection of the same strange birds circling over them, like vultures waiting for the leftovers!

Still dripping wet and by now a little chilly, Elvie began to regret her impulsive decision to retrieve the scale, and worried as to what would happen next on their crazy quest. They both sat silently on the river bank as the eerie birds circled above. Once again, Aiden put his arm around Elvie to comfort her.

'It'll be alright!' he said hopefully.

'I would like to believe that dragons don't exist,' said Elvie snapping angrily, 'but so far, everything I thought didn't exist – clearly does!' She had begun to understand that magic meant anything was possible. The children sat silently. The hot sun warmed them and quickly started to dry Elvie's clothes. The heat of the rays on their skin helped them to calm down a little.

'It's nice here!' she said wistfully as she relaxed in the sun with the river bubbling past.

'Yes, but we need to find out why everyone is in a dream!' Aiden reminded her.

'And what those birds are up to?' replied Elvie 'they're creepy!' A sudden gust of wind chilled them and they huddled closer for warmth. The grey birds frantically flapped and squawked, then hurriedly flew away.

'Thank goodness!' said Elvie relieved that the horrible birds had gone.

A short while later Aiden and Elvie felt the wind had changed direction and become more rhythmical. Steady, warm gusts, were rasping from behind them. Turning to see why, both children gasped and fell backwards in shock and fear. Standing on two legs, and now only ten feet away from them at the edge of the river, stood a terrifying bird-like creature the size of an elephant. Its back, long lizard like neck and folded wings were covered in thick overlapping rock-like golden scales. Armoured skin, thick and black, protected its bony head, its strong muscular legs, deep chest and sturdy broad tail. The children fell to the ground as the creature turned its head towards them. It was staring at them while deep rumblings and snorts came from its nose. Petrified, the children couldn't move from where they had fallen. The beast lumbered towards them, slowly and heavily, carefully placing its bony black feet on the rocky sand of the riverside. To counterbalance, as it faltered slightly on some rocks, it confidently lifted an impressively huge pair of golden scaly wings, revealing the rough jet hide of its underbelly. The scales clattered against each other as it outstretched its wings. It was a magnificent dragon!

'AAAHH'! Screamed Elvie as the beast got closer. She tried to scramble away from it, but her legs felt like they had disappeared!

Aiden bravely jumped in front of his sister to protect her from the dragon, standing tall to face it with nothing but an outstretched arm and fist. Clouding the sun, the beast's wings cast a shadow that completely enveloped the children. As it came closer and closer, they were engulfed by the smell of hot rock dust. Breathing in deeply, the beast expanded its enormous chest.

'This is the end!' thought Aiden, still courageously holding his ground, with his fist held out, as if to take on the dragon in a straightforward fight.

The beast began to exhale, the children ducked, waiting for their final moments on this Earth. They were expecting to be engulfed in fire, but instead it let out a rumble from its mouth. The rumble turned into a murmur and the dragon loudly boomed out in a gravelly bold voice.

'STAND DOWN!' The force knocked Aiden and Elvie to the ground. They both fell in a jumble of twisted arms and legs.

'You are the "Bold One" you are the "True One"!' said the beast, rasping directly at each child in turn. Astonished, they pulled themselves together and gasping in relief at not being eaten or cooked alive, the children stood up and brushed themselves off whilst still keeping one eye on the dragon's movements.

Aiden took the lead, and said gutsily, 'I am Aiden and this is my sister Elvie,' wondering what the beast meant by the "Bold one" and "True one"?!

'Do not fear me,' snorted the dragon, 'you have finally called me back to Sreen after the longest sleep. I am Auric, Rock Dragon of Sreen, I am here after so long, to help you put things in this world back to how they should be.' It said solemnly, rasping and puffing from the sides of his cheeks.

The realisation that this *was* happening to them, and they *were* expected to do something enormous for this world, had hit the children quite hard. The sudden appearance of the dragon had initially terrified them as they believed they were going to be attacked or eaten alive by him!

'I need to sit down!' said Elvie, quite exhausted.

She found a convenient bolder to perch on, put her head in her hands and tried to rest her mind.

'Rest is what we all need now,' rumbled Auric from the depths of his chest. 'I have been sleeping for hundreds of years, and for the moment, I find simple movement and speech tiring. Tomorrow, I will be recovered! Tonight, we will talk of your quest, I will listen to your account so far, and then we shall all rest.'

With that he clanked and clattered around in a circle and wrapped his tail around himself. He eventually came to rest on a comfortable patch of ground. It reminded the children of a dog lying down – A very big dog! Once he had finally got settled, he urged the children to talk of their adventure. They found him strangely kind and understanding, and were greatly relieved that they could seem to relax with him after such a shaky start.

With their new found trust, they spent all afternoon telling Auric of their tales; of arriving at Umble Down, of Tag and the magical map, of the missing "Mirror Diamond", the fading magic, the strange grey birds, and finally, of the sleepy Twilks. Auric lay with one eye open, perfectly still but for the pointed end of his tail plate slowly lifting and lowering, in response to the children's words.

With a loud and weary yawn, he said, 'Tomorrow, when we are all rested, I will tell you all I know,' and without waiting for a reply, he fell fast asleep. Tired, and quite bewildered by such a very strange day, the children ate the last of the food from their backpacks. They found strange comfort – and finally sleep – curled up in the warm arc of the body, of a huge dragon they now knew as Auric!

Chapter 7

The Truth Revealed

Dawn broke around them in beautiful shimmering emerald hues.

'Wake Up', Auric hissed. Aiden and Elvie, both having slept well, rubbed their eyes and yawned. Not yet fully awake, they were lightly jolted by Auric moving position as he started to stand. Hastily, they jumped to their feet, so as not to be squashed. Auric's skin rippled, and his legs crunched and clanked him to his feet.

The sun was just beginning to rise over the crater now in shades of orange and yellow, which glistened on Auric's golden wings. He confidently swished his tail through a tall leafy bush nearby, which sent a cluster of ripe, round, yellow fruit to the ground.

'Eat,' he rumbled, 'these will suit your stomachs.'

The children rushed to the fruit as if never having eaten before. Biting through, they found them very refreshing.

'Mmm, like lemony-apply-pears.' Said Elvie relieved to be having some breakfast.

Aiden, still with juice dripping from his chin, looked worried after thoughtlessly gorging himself. 'Are they safe?' he begged Auric.

The Dragon kindly smiled as only a dragon can, wrinkling the corner of his leathery mouth. 'Not only safe, but delicious too' he replied, eating some himself. He then stood to face the children to get their full attention.

'It is my turn to speak,' he said sincerely. 'You have told me that you already know of the dragon wars and about this evil Ilex,' he said solemnly. 'You tell me of the fading magic of Sreen and of the pressing need to find the missing "Mirror Diamond" – to mend the magic.' He paused thoughtfully. 'You tell me of a magical map, and of an elder Twilk called Tag. You also tell me that King Neema and Queen Amari are being kept safely at Umble Down Castle,' he paused again, this time demanding the childrens' direct attention. 'I give you the dragon's word of truth – for this is all we can speak. Our hearts are honest, and so are our actions.' Candidly, he carried on, 'what you tell me is very worrying for every world on this planet, and for every magical realm.'

'There are more worlds like this?' questioned Aiden.

'That will become clearer to you as you grow older and stronger, and as you experience more.' explained Auric, knowingly.

'So, getting back to now!' said Elvie hastily, 'why are you worried?' she asked.

'I am worried because there is no natural reason for the magic to fade,' he said aghast, 'all Twilks are powerful enough to mend it!' he rasped his words, as the children listened and tried to make sense of what he was saying. What's more,' he said angrily, 'the dragons did not die – we cannot! We just sleep until it is our time again, and that time is now!' He gestured with his wing to himself. Sounding irate by now, he added, 'The evil Ilex only disappeared, supposedly never to be found again – he surely did not die! Rumour had it that he had become dangerous, and eventually gone quite mad!' Calming down a little, he continued. 'The dragon's gem, "Mirror Diamond", was retrieved by us in the war. Ilex was sloppy and arrogant. He left it unguarded, so the last few dragons took it back and hid it! This was to stop greed or evil destroying weaker beings like Twilk again!' he said defensively. 'It can only be found by a brave heart, and a pure & honest soul.'

Trying to make sense of it all, Aiden said 'but you destroyed the mountain!'

'Yes, the war was devastating and foolish,' said Auric, his head bowed with shame. 'So, all the remaining dragons realised their wrong doing and decided to hide the diamond to keep it safe. We have waited until the time was right to make amends, and to help restore the balance between good and evil.' He explained that the dragons of Sreen are formed from the atoms that make the elements; Air, Water, Fire and Earth. 'We sleep every few thousand years, to help stay hidden and safe from trouble. We really don't like to fight!' he said. 'Sleeping is to become one with our elements – we are nourished this way.'

'Well, if dragons hid the diamond in the first place, why don't they know where it is now?' asked Aiden intelligently.

'A couple of hundred years asleep is an awfully long time, even for a dragon!' Auric replied, by now sounding slightly awkward and embarrassed. He eventually admitted (confessed) that they had forgotten where they had left it!? 'And anyway, we are magical beasts in our own right. We don't need it to *make* our magic' he added, in an attempt to regain some superiority!

'So, the myth of retrieving the diamond, to mend magic, is untrue?' questioned Elvie.

Aiden felt shocked, as he realised he had been lied to. Angrily he said, 'So, Tag is a liar! What about the map, why would he give it to us, if he didn't want to help save the magic?' He realised things just weren't adding up. 'It's a lie that Sreen magic is fading then.' He was feeling used.

'The magic *is* fading.' replied Auric, 'but not for the reasons your friend Tag has given you!' he said, adding 'I don't remember this elder, Tag?'

'Double OH NO!' shrieked Elvie, who was by now feeling very insecure about the whole situation they had found themselves in.

'Tag said Twilks hadn't learned magic since the war! He said that only the elder's knew magic and it was forbidden to be taught because of the risk of it being used for bad!' Auric explained that magic, to a Twilk on Sreen, was like breathing, it happened naturally, it didn't need to be taught, just respected and nurtured.

Elvie asked thoughtfully 'Are we under a magic spell, only Tag told us that he had cloaked us in magic and that would stop us being seen!'

'I sense no magic around you.' replied Auric wisely.

Aiden, realising where Elvie was coming from, added, 'So why didn't any of the Twilks see us, and why were they all half asleep?' Auric, intrigued by their question, gave it some thought.

After some time, he answered 'Dewberry magic, enchantment – it is enchantment!' he frowned.

Elvie took from her pocket some forgotten about Dewberries she had picked the day before. 'These?!' she asked, holding them up to Auric.

'Yes, we dragons use them to help our young to sleep,' he said, 'but to add them to a magical potion is heavy, dangerous magic indeed. These plants are as old as time, and therefore carry the knowledge of the universe and all magic in their fruits.' He frowned again and added worriedly, 'It is very powerful enchantment indeed. I think the Twilk must have been under its spell for many, many years!'

'So, someone has enchanted *all* the Twilks!' Elvie was now feeling quite frightened, 'I thought they had all been drinking slumber cup liquor?' she added.

'I think Tag has some questions to answer!' Aiden was angry and he wanted to know the truth.

The sun was now high above them and the day was bright, but a gloomy mood hung over the children. Auric sidled noisily up to them.

'You must remember,' he said wisely, 'you are the "Bold One", and you are the "True One"! This means that magic has chosen you to save this land one way or another. It is your destiny to be here, and I am here to help you. You were able to pull my scale from the river! You are here to give Sreen back to the Twilks!'

'I feel so much better now!' said Aiden sarcastically.

'That's more like it, some spirit!' replied Auric, not noticing the lack of sincerity in Aiden's words. 'Now show me that map!' he rumbled. Speedily, Aiden took the map out of his bag, and as usual it unfurled in front of him, but this time it was just a plain map with no visions or voices! Auric leaned forward and sniffed the paper.

'Hmmm' he grumbled roughly, 'describe this *Tag*?' he asked suspiciously.

'That's easy, he looks like all Twilks.' Elvie replied. 'He is very thin, with long arms and legs, but he's a lot older than most of the others. And..., he has a very large bulbous nose!'

'Oh, and green eyes,' added Aiden.

'Green you say?' Auric paused, sifting through his memories, 'but all Twilks have blue eyes,' he said suspiciously. 'Only those Twilk who are near to death, or who have gone mad – only their eyes turn green.' He added gravely. 'I have lived for thousands of years and seen many Twilk born, age and die. They usually live long and fruitful lives, between one hundred and two hundred years, sometimes more. When they die, they move into the magic, and become one with all things. I have only known of one Twilk who has gone mad!'

'Don't tell me, that one is Ilex!' said Aiden, hoping he was wrong, but still in some disbelief.

'So, you're saying that Tag is Ilex' Elvie queried, 'but he was so nice to us!' she added, sad and confused.

'I don't believe he is near death, because if he were, he would be too weak to use magic!' added Aiden, confirming that Tag was indeed Ilex.

'I'd recognise that foul smell anywhere,' growled Auric. 'His Scent is all over that map.' Astonished, confused and betrayed, the children slowly understood that their calling, to save the magic of Sreen, was becoming a more complicated quest!

'So, just to make sure I'm on the same wave length as all of you, TAG IS ILEX!?' Elvie reiterated loudly.

'As sure as I'm a dragon!' replied Auric. 'Magic has summoned you to our land to help free us from this evil once and for all,' he said, 'if you can do this, all dragon species, be they Earth, Water, Fire or Air, will be able and happy to live on Sreen with all Twilk'.

'It was an odd way of calling us!' added Elvie.

'Ilex must have intercepted the magic as it brought you here!' replied Auric. 'That way he could take control and get you to retrieve the diamond for himself without suspicion. He will now know that I have been called, because the Tarks will have told him!'

'What are Tarks?' asked Aiden.

'They are magically made birds. I noticed them around you when I arrived back in Sreen. Things made from bad magic are called Cigams, and so the Tarks are also Cigams. They are dark, and could only be made from bad thoughts!' added Auric with some seriousness. Looking up at the sky, they all noticed that more large patches of magic were now fading, and alarmingly, so was the sun.

Auric explained in more detail. 'Ilex is draining all the magic from the Twilk and is drawing it to him. That is why it is fading. Twilk can't fight him while half asleep. His intention is to get the diamond and to use its power to help fix the hole in magic. That way he has complete power over everyone, as the enchantment will stay forever!'

'We have to stop him!' said Aiden determined to put things right, and feeling very cheated!

'Should we stop looking for the diamond and just let it stay hidden?' asked Elvie.

'No' replied Auric justly, 'Ilex will always keep on looking until he succeeds, and that will make things far worse for everyone. When you have the diamond, it will be safe because you are the "True One". That will be the beginning of control, and the beginning of the end of Ilex's power!' He made sure that Elvie was looking directly at him and said, 'your task is clear Elvie. It's you who must find the "Mirror Diamond"!'

He turned to look at Aiden, who by now knew exactly what was coming. 'And you Aiden, your task is to find and capture Ilex!' he rumbled confidently and continued to rasp more instructions to both children. 'Aiden, your courage will guide you, and your determination will strengthen you!' he was calm and inspiring, 'you will go on a nimble leg carrier for speed, and be protected by a trusted woofnsnapper! I have already summoned them.' His voice was very firm. Aiden just looked at Elvie and raised an eyebrow, as if to say that he thought Auric was being a bit dramatic!

'Elvie' Auric spoke seriously, although his eyes shone kindly at her. '*You* will find the diamond, and I have something to help you,' he gestured with his head for them to stand back and began to inhale deeply. Both children rushed backwards, knowing what was about to happen. With that, Auric, aiming at the pebbles on the ground between them, exhaled a fire bolt from his mouth. The pebbles glowed red under the flame, and stayed red long after he had stopped.

'I am giving you an extremely rare dream weevil' he said, feeling quite pleased with himself, as he stared at the pebbles. The children followed his gaze.

'What are we looking for?' asked Aiden, but before Auric could answer, one of the pebbles the size of a pea turned a vivid green in front of their eyes! It sprouted thin black legs and a long black head and nose. Auric's tail flicked around and scooped it up. He passed it to Elvie. She took it gingerly in her hand. It turned bright pink, and started to click rapidly at her.

'It likes you!' observed Auric, 'he knows you are true!'

'What do I do with him, and how will he help me?' asked Elvie, quite puzzled.

'He will...' but this time, before Auric could finish, the dream weevil had darted along Elvie's arm, skipped up her neck and into her ear. All the while Elvie squirmed fidgeted and laughed out loud as the others looked on.

'It tickles!' she laughed.

'Try to be still and he will settle.' Auric advised. Breathing deeply, and wrapping her arms around her body, she eventually managed to just about stay still and quiet. Slowly, her breathing came back to normal and all was calm.

'He will give you guidance – just ask him what you want to know!' Auric told her. Shortly after, although still looking a little bewildered, the lights went out on Elvie and she dropped into her brother's arms in a deep sleep.

'It will pass!' said Auric calmly, as Aiden carefully laid his sister on a patch of grass. The dream weevil left her ear and scurried off into the rocks as Auric explained further.

'They are all knowing, and are formed from the ancient elements. They can live for millennia, and only speak to a "True One". He will have psychic contact with her in the form of visions and words. To know *anything,* all she needs to do is ask!' Lying down next to her on the ground to protect her, Auric grated out the words, 'rest now – Elvie can sleep it off while we wait for your ride and protection!' he rippled and clanked into a comfortable position. Seeing Aiden's worried look, as he tucked his snout under his tail, he added in a muffled voice, 'she will be fine!' then he closed his eyes and instantly slept. Thinking about Auric's words, Aiden simply sat and stared at the river. He hoped he could find the courage and strength to succeed in his challenge!

Chapter 8

A Brave Fight

Elvie awoke smiling. Her head was as clear as it had ever been. She felt as if the cobwebs had been dusted from her mind. Aiden had been getting acquainted with his nimble leg carrier and woofnsnapper. These peculiar creatures had arrived earlier, while Elvie still slept.

Aiden gestured towards an extremely thin and long, four-legged horse like creature. It was hairless, apart from its long (shaggy), silver main and tail.

'Meet Fly!' he said proudly, smoothing the beast's soft grey skin with his hand. Fly turned his thin bony head and nuzzled Aiden's back.

'He is very handsome, but he does look a bit too small for you' remarked Elvie doubtfully.

Auric intervened, 'He has been chosen for his strength and speed.' He explained that Fly was used to pulling and carrying heavy loads at speed.

Elvie got up to give her big brother a hug. She felt light and quite happy inside. Reaching her arms out for him, she was suddenly stopped in her tracks by a set of snarling, gnashing, doglike teeth. The things legs stood rigid on its spindly but strong paws as it stood denying anyone passage. Gasping, she quickly stepped back.

'Meet Buckler,' smiled Aiden impishly, 'no really, I mean it, come over and stroke him, he really is quite friendly!'

Bravely but ever so slowly, Elvie moved towards the black and tan creature. It too was very slim, with long legs.

'Like everything else on Sreen!' thought Elvie. It was covered with short rough fur that parted in different directions, like rosettes. The creature bowed its head in submission, and rubbed its stubby soft ear on her leg, below the knee.

'Is he going to defend you?' she asked worriedly, 'only he doesn't look very big and strong – does he?'

'He *is* going to protect me!' replied Aiden confidently.

'Well, he is quite scary at first' Elvie said, giggling as Buckler licked her hand.

Auric grumbled impatiently 'We must hurry now, Ilex is on our tails. We have to be one step ahead of him to bring about his downfall. The Tarks will have told him by now that we are working together. He will fear his plan may fail, which will make him angrier and more destructive!'

Suddenly Elvie gasped, 'I can see the diamond inside my head now, I KNOW WHERE IT IS!' she screeched excitedly.

'Stop!.' Auric commanded. 'Say nothing more. We must let Aiden go to capture Ilex without knowing where the diamond is. That way, Ilex cannot magically read his mind.' He continued, 'you must guide me Elvie, and together we will go to find "Mirror Diamond"!'

With that, Aiden, full of determination and energy, threw his backpack (map inside), over his shoulder. He mounted Fly and together they sped off. He had no idea what was going to happen, but he had a deep belief that he would succeed.

'Trust me Sis!' he called out, his head turned behind him, 'I feel it will be OK!' They quickly covered the ground, up the side of the crater towards Umble down, with buckler at their side.

'Be safe!' Elvie said, worried for her brother. Both children by now had forgotten about their normal lives back home. They were now part of Sreen!

'Climb on my back' rasped Auric, 'we must be off!'

Grappling to get up, Elvie wondered why she had got the taller, bigger, and much scarier ride. Auric guided her feet with his scaly golden wings, until she found a comfortable position to sit. His skin was so thick, and she was so light, that he felt nothing; she was like a feather to him.

'Hold on around my neck,' he rumbled. She grasped hold quickly and firmly, wedging her feet in between his scales. Wrapping her arms around his leathery neck, she fixed her fingers on the ridges of rough, armoured skin. His huge golden wings stretched outwards as he bent his legs and pushed gently upwards. Gracefully and smoothly, they were airborne and rising high above the crater.

Leaning as far forward as she could without losing her grip, Elvie whispered to Auric, 'we need to go to Umble Over!'

They climbed higher and higher into the sky. The once green clouds were now a shimmering gold from the reflection of the sun, and they parted in wisps as Auric's wings beat through them. Below and to their left, they could see Umble Down Castle glistening in the distance. Ahead, were the dark cliffs of the Grey Ledge Mountains, which formed the entrance to Great Twilk Pass. Owned by King Neema and Queen Amari, these mountains had been mined for hundreds of years to extract the wonderful Star Gems, which all Twilks used as currency.

'The map told me of the gems, but not how they are made. Do you know?'

Elvie asked Auric.

'It is believed that their 'Star Gems' are made by the rain washing stardust from the sky. Once trapped in the rocks, and over thousands of years, the dust forms into crystals. Usually, they are star shaped, but they can occasionally be round or even square!' recounted Auric.

'Is most of the information that we have been given by the map true, or are we being misled by it?' Elvie wanted to stop feeling unsure of her new knowledge about Sreen.

'The map began its life as a normal map. This will always be its true essence, even when used by dark magic. It will only be able to show its truth, and so can be helpful to Aiden. However, it can be used as a magical tool to guide its owner. *This* is how Ilex is using it. He is magically connected to it. This, along with the Tarks, will help him know its whereabouts and therefore, the whereabouts of whoever is carrying it.'

Meanwhile, on *his* journey, Aiden had time to ponder how he was going to capture Ilex. He didn't really have a clue! All he could do was trust that it would happen. As he and Fly were galloping along, he felt the strength and power emanating from the creature under him. 'Such purpose!' thought Aiden, about his nimble leg carrier. Presently, he found himself remembering what Auric had told him. His courage would guide him – and his determination would make him strong. Making full use of Fly's example and of Auric's words, Aiden dug deep into his being. 'I can do this,' he said to himself, which made the adrenaline surge inside his body and his heart beat faster. He had somehow found more courage and confidence to get the job done!

With renewed determination, he squeezed his legs around Fly to make him go even faster. They galloped tirelessly, thrashing and crashing through bushes and over difficult terrain, carefully avoiding the road so as not to be noticed from the castle. With Buckler by their side, sometimes taking the lead, or dropping back if he sensed danger, Aiden felt comfortable as if riding on air, or like being at one with speed itself.

Power surged through him as they arrived at Feather Fuzzy Fields. The journey had charged him with energy. Buckler was already on guard, not leaving Aiden's side but constantly looking around and sniffing the air for danger. Dismounting Fly, Aiden heard a loud 'SQUAWK.' Looking up, he could see three Tarks circling above in the sky. All around him there was silence, not a Twilk to be seen. The map surprisingly began to rustle and push about in his rucksack, as if it were trying to escape.

'He knows I'm here!' thought Aiden, looking about the empty place. At that very moment, a silvery, shimmering light appeared at the foot of Middle Big Hill. Aiden stood tall, ready for anything. Along the path to Umble Down Castle, and through the mist, suddenly appeared the unmistakably creepy figure of Ilex. He wore dark clothes, which gave him a confident and somewhat menacing appearance.

'Ha, formerly known as Tag!..' Aiden sarcastically thought to himself. Buckler rumbled a low threatening growl and coiled his body, ready to pounce. Irritated by Ilex's deception, Aiden shouted out angrily.

'I KNOW IT ALL DECEIVER. YOU ARE THE EVIL ILEX!' As he spoke, he could feel his anger building up inside him. It made him feel strong. 'You have used us to satisfy your greed. We will not let you succeed in destroying your own people!' he said boldly.

'Brave words!' replied Ilex. 'I felt your strength when we first met, and I knew you were the right choice to help me!' he scoffed.

'Help *you*, I don't think so – not now!' snapped Aiden.

Ilex laughed madly. 'Mwahahahaa, you have already helped me enormously!' he said provoking Aiden with his words. 'By awakening a dragon, though quite unexpected by me, you've boosted the magic of Sreen, allowing me to channel even more magic!' he said wickedly. He lifted his arms upwards, hands towards the sky, his eyes rolled back in their sockets. Electric blue arrows and sparks of energy surged from the sky into his hands and body, piercing and fizzing as he absorbed the magic. He could taste the energy, and sucked it into his mouth, through his teeth, and over his tongue. 'I can feel your sister getting closer to the diamond!' he teased.

Incensed by this, Aiden ran at Ilex, ready to tackle him to the ground. Ilex powerfully deflected the attack with a shimmering magical shield, and Aiden fell to the floor. Buckler charged Ilex and snapped furiously at his feet, one at a time, making him hop from leg to leg! Angered by this, Ilex shot a bolt of magic at him, which easily flicked the woofnsnapper away. He yelped, but bravely got up and charged again, snarling and snapping.

'YOU WILL NEVER STOP ME....THE POWER OF THE MAGIC IS MINE' roared Ilex, striking the creature once more.

Aiden stood strong. Ilex's words sparked a thought in his head. 'If magic belongs to Ilex, and the map is made by bad magic, then not only is the map a Cigam, but it's a powerful link to Ilex's energy. That must be why at the beginning of all this, when I knew him as Tag, he warned us not to let it get into the *wrong* hands!' To buy himself more time to think clearly, Aiden quickly dropped to the floor and rolled behind a pile of rocks. 'If I destroy the map,' he thought, 'I may be able to weaken Ilex.' Crouching behind the rock, he quickly removed the map from his bag. Holding it firmly, he moved out into the open. He blatantly goaded Ilex by shaking it at him. The map squirmed in his hands, trying to get away. 'Open!' shouted Aiden. It obeyed and spread out. Aiden grabbed at the opposite edges, as if to rip it into pieces.

'Oh, I'm so scared,' mocked Ilex. Then he shot a dart of potent blue magic directly at Aiden. It missed the boy's body as he dodged to the left, but it hit his right hand.

'UGH!' shouted Aiden painfully, but the magic dart had made him drop the map. Ilex seized the opportunity, and reaching his hands out in front of him, he magically drew the map towards him.

'I'm too strong for you!' he sneered, laughing at the stricken boy.

Wanting to charge Ilex, but not knowing whether it would do any good, Aiden's frustration and anger began to boil over. With this came a new determination. Remembering Auric's words, he found himself focusing his mind on destroying the map. His courage, as Auric had predicted, helped him. He stood tall, facing Ilex, not quivering. He had found his power! All he knew in his mind was that this had to be the end of the map!

Energy surged through his body, building within him as if he were about to explode. Its force was strong, something he had never felt before as it rumbled turbulently through him. His only intention was to destroy the map. A wave of energy suddenly pulsed through him. He raised his arm, and shockingly, out of his hand he threw a lightning bolt. It darted through the air and hit the map, closely followed by another and yet another. Both of his hands were now throwing bolts of lightning, one after the other. The map hissed as it was engulfed in flames and turned to ash.

Both Aiden and Ilex were stunned. Neither had expected that! Aiden fell to the ground. Ilex screamed in disbelief as his treasured map turned to ashes in front of his eyes. He had completely underestimated Aiden's strength and power.

'NO... NO.... NO......' Ilex raged, staring at the pile of dust in front of him. He fell to his knees, holding his head in his hands and sobbing loudly.

A wave of energy, like that from an explosion, suddenly boomed across the land. Tarks fell from the sky as harmless handfuls of dust. The map had been more magical than Aiden had realised. Destroying it had broken the Dewberry Slumber spell. He seemed to understand now, that destroying something made of dark magic somehow causes a vacuum, which in turn, sucks more dark magic and negative energy into itself. In effect it implodes leaving pure and positive energy.

Coming to his senses, and now knowing he was strong enough, Aiden – Buckler at his side – rushed over and grabbed the defeated Ilex. Weakened and demoralised, Ilex didn't even try to slither away!

* * *

Chapter 9

Saving the Magic

Elvie, using her intuition, had guided Auric to a particular spot at the southeast of Grey Ledge Mountains near Umble Over.

'Down here!' she called. Slowly, they glided downwards, circling through the clouds to find a safe place to land. 'HERE!' she shouted, pointing to a small woodland clearing next to a tiny Grickle wood cottage.

'Hold tight!' rumbled Auric.

It felt to Elvie, as if they were falling straight down. Her pulse raced and her stomach flipped over inside her. Auric turned his great wings downwards, pushing against the air and using its force as a brake. He gently bent his knees as they landed quietly and softly, next to a large patch of whistle weed.

Having seen this place in her vision was one thing, but to actually be there for real was amazing.

'Wow, this place is simply stunning,' she declared to Auric.

The grass in the clearing was a vivid green against the darkness of the surrounding trees. Subtle whistling sounds were emanating from the purple tufty heads of the tall Whistleweed that was swaying in the breeze. Harmony butterflies flitted around, their wings making musical notes with every beat, and changing colour with every note. The scent of the Whistleweed was intoxicating. Elvie felt like she was in heaven, as if peace had swept over her, she wanted to stay forever! It was bewitching!

'Stay on track!' Auric grumbled, as he noticed Elvie's thoughts drifting. His words jolted her back to her task. To retrieve the diamond! She clambered down from Auric, her legs and arms stiff from the journey on the back of a large dragon! The soft, short grass under her feet felt springy, as if it had recently been cut. As she looked around, she noticed a small flock of Yooze were chomping their way across the clearing.

'They look bizarre!' she thought to herself, wondering how they grew such brightly coloured fleeces. 'At least they keep the grass short,' she thought, and then realised she was day dreaming again! 'I think the whistle weed scent is making me lose concentration!' she announced to Auric.

The lumbering beast wisely answered. 'Close your eyes and look to your inner self. Try to use your connection with the dream weevil. You will be able to sense your way to "Mirror Diamond".' Doing as she was told, she closed her eyes. Although everything about her situation was unfamiliar, she felt confident that something good would happen. She was right. She immediately began to feel calmer, as if her mind was filtering out all unnecessary thoughts. Yes, she could actually feel like she was in control of herself, strong and calm. A deep sense of knowing came over her.

'It's not far away, but I sense it is deep in the ground!' she told Auric. Suddenly, she saw a flash of light inside her head. Gasping and stumbling, she fell on her hands and knees to brace herself, as a vision of Aiden played out in her head. 'It's Aiden!' she said, quite alarmed, 'He's fighting Ilex as we speak. He's using magic too!' She was shocked, but proud of her brother's new found skill and ability.

'Good news!' replied Auric, wrinkling the soft corners of his mouth and smiling. The bold one has found his inner magic!' he stated triumphantly. 'Now – to the diamond – we must retrieve it before all magic fades.' He said seriously, and reminding her of her tasks ahead.

Elvie looked around them and noticed for the first time that the cottage was derelict. 'In my vision, it is close to blast stone!' she said, searching the undergrowth and overgrown garden of the Grickle wood cottage. To the far left of the cottage, about fifteen feet away, was a large tangled knot of vine. It looked suspiciously like a man-made regular shape. 'Over there!' she directed Auric to it, pointing with her finger. Auric sniffed around the area cautiously. He began to tear away at the vine with his talons, exposing an old blast stone well. It stood about four feet high, and was no more than four feet in diameter around the inside wall.

'Yes – this must be it.' Elvie excitedly reached over the edge with her arms, balancing her chest on the rock to stop her from falling in. She paused for a few seconds to clear her mind and to try and concentrate. 'I believe the diamond is down there!' she said, feeling its magical pull, as she stared down into the blackness. The well was just rocks and a hole, there wasn't a winch handle. 'The Twilks must have pulled the water up by hand!' she said, noticing an old wooden bucket and a rotten frayed rope lying on the ground beside it.

'You must trust in yourself, as your brother has told you Elvie!' said Auric.

'That means I have got to go down there doesn't it?'
she replied nervously.

The well felt so small and narrow. Reaching in over the edge into the darkness, she noticed the inner walls appeared to be dry, not slimy, as she first imagined. She knew she had to get in and do it quickly.

'Focus!' she said to herself out loud, looking for another way. The thought suddenly jumped into her mind, that because of her psychic link to the diamond, she might be able to summon it to her. 'I will try and call the diamond to me!' she announced stubbornly. Closing her eyes and quietening her mind once more, she concentrated on the diamond, its shape, its colour, its energy and..., suddenly there was a distant clicking, buzzing and fluttering from within the well. It became louder and louder as a surprising echoey rush of sounds came from inside. Elvie darted out of the way, just in time too, as a flurry of clattering black and violet beetles swarmed out of the well, buzzing and swirling past her head. They came to rest as a group, on the roof of the old cottage, causing the illusion of a hole where they had landed. 'That's it!' Elvie said, staring down the well, which was by now only four feet deep and much brighter. 'I had forgotten about the Abyss Beetle in my vision. They can make a light place look really deep and dark. They've been keeping guard over the precious diamond ever since it was left here all those years ago.' Wasting no more time, she leapt into the well. Crouching on the floor, her eyes scoured the inside wall, and there, set just like one of the blast stones of the wall, was; the "Mirror Diamond"! Carefully, she eased it out of its resting place, and still crouching, dragged it onto her legs. It was very heavy!

Auric turned and lowered his muscular tail down into the well. There was just enough space, and with one final effort, Elvie managed to slide the diamond onto the dragon's spearhead shaped tail plate. Effortlessly and safely, Auric lifted the diamond out of the well and set it down on the grass. Elvie, by now dazed and exhausted, hurriedly clambered out of the well. Without warning, there was a mighty boom in the air. Their ears jangled, and Elvie dropped to her knees, as a shockwave of electric blue energy crossed the sky.

'HE'S DONE IT!' shouted Elvie excitedly, 'AIDEN HAS DEFEATED ILEX.!'

'So have we!' Auric stated, looking at the wonderful diamond on the ground in front of him. Elvie and Auric felt the land around them and under their feet rumble as the bad magic was being expelled. Full of dynamic spirit and keen to see her brother, she managed to quickly secure the diamond to Auric's shoulders with whistle weed. She jumped effortlessly onto his back, dug her toes in between his scales, and they were off!

Excitedly she said, 'Hurry, I must get to see Aiden, he's a hero!'

With that, Auric rose into the sky, and speedily they took off in the direction of Umble Down Castle. Elvie, once again, clinging on to the dragon's neck, but happily enjoying the spectacular scenery.

***

Aiden was by now being assisted by plenty of extremely grateful and free Twilks. They were hugely relieved that the spell had at last been broken. Ilex's hands were tied tightly behind his back by one Twilk and he was strapped to a large wooden pole by another. The pole was supported on either end by two more gleeful Twilks, who carried him to the castle.

Looking up, as the holes in the sky began to heal, Aiden saw Auric, Elvie, and the diamond arrive safely at the castle. At the same moment, the Royal Twilks were leaving their castle imprisonment for the first time since the enchantment had begun. The dragon's skilful landing had caused the air to gust over the onlookers, blowing their hair into their faces. Elvie, helped by Aiden, climbed down from Auric's strong back. There were by now, plenty of friendly Twilk at hand and they were practically tripping over themselves to be helpful. While untying the diamond, Elvie noticed how beautiful the Twilk were as a people.

'Such elegant limbs and beautiful features,' she thought. 'The enchantment took all that away from them. How wicked Ilex was to do that to anybody!'

Aiden and Elvie, closely followed by Auric, carried the diamond towards King Neema and Queen Amari. The look of joy on the faces of the Royal Twilks was something that the children would never forget.

'To show our eternal gratitude!' announced King Neema, 'and if Auric is in agreement?,'(he looked kindly at the dragon, who instantly nodded his head to signal that he knew what the King was about to say), 'we would like to set "Mirror Diamond" in the walls of Umble Down Castle as a beacon of good. It will remind *all* to treat others how we would want to be treated in return.' The King's wise words were cheered and applauded loudly by all the Twilks. Auric knew that by making this decision, the Royals were not only empowering their own people, but also inviting all the banished dragon species back to Sreen!

'Of course, we would not have been rescued,' King Neema continued, 'without the immense courage and honesty of our new human friends, Aiden and Elvie. For this, we are truly and eternally grateful!' and he clapped in the direction of the two children who both blushed and beamed enormous smiles, feeling very proud of their achievements!

Queen Amari now addressed both the children directly. 'The new found gifts you have will stay with you forever. You will be surprised how often you may need them in your future adventures,' she gently added, 'is there anything we can give you in return to show our appreciation?' She held out her fine, orange silk covered arm and revealed a sparkling jewel decorated hand. She touched the children's lowered heads in turn – She was truly and breathtakingly elegant!

Turning their heads and nodding at each other in agreement, the children gracefully curtsied and bowed, and answered simultaneously, 'To come back!', Aiden added 'whenever we want to, please Your Majesty?!'

Queen Amari gave them a knowing look and replied wisely, 'That ability is already destined for you.'

Giving an unheard of embrace to each child, which felt awkward as the children were so large compared with the Twilks, King Neema and Queen Amari regally bid them goodbye with a bow and slow nod of the head. They then went about the task of finally imprisoning Ilex for good, in the castle dungeons.

The Twilks celebrated joyfully, with magical music from instruments made from all manner of natural things. There were seed drums, pod guitars, and beautifully hand carved wooden wind instruments. They drank blue tan liquor and ate fresh fruit and specially prepared cakes, as if they hadn't eaten before. The children knew the party would go on for days!!!....

'It's time to go home!' said Elvie, happily looking around at the cheerful and colourful Twilk people. She gazed at the beautifully mystical sky, the mended magic, and the vibrant glow now settling over the magical land of Sreen. Turning to say goodbye to Auric, the children felt a familiar buzzing in their heads...

***

Quite abruptly, they were all at once back in the woods by their den, at home. Realising where she was,

Elvie sighed, 'I didn't get to say goodbye' and a tear formed in her eye at the separation from their new found and very large friend.

'My watch says we've only been gone for two hours!' said Aiden, stunned at how much they got done in that time. 'I can't believe what we did,' he said, 'I think this is the start of a fantastic new life for us.' He felt his new found confidence brimming up inside him.

Elvie was already reminiscing about their amazing adventures. She found herself wondering if or how they would ever really be able to find their way back to the magical land of Sreen? Smiling with glee, she looked into Aiden's cheerful and innocent face as she pulled from her trouser pocket – two delicious Dewberries and a shimmering, golden dragon scale!

***

(to be continued)

Fay Jones.

Fay spent her early career working in the healing arts. Nowadays, she enjoys creating her own artwork and writing and publishing short stories for children. She gains her inspiration from her family and the natural world.

Fay's other creations can be found on her website at:

www.fayjones.net

please feel free to leave a review of this book on the website, or with Facebook or Amazon.